OCT   2005

JE
Inches, Alison.
Hooray for Polka Dots!

Hooray for Polka Dots!

by Alison Inches
illustrated by Ian Chernichaw

Ready-to-Read

Simon Spotlight / Nick Jr.

New York   London   Toronto   Sydney

Based on the TV series *Blue's Clues*® created by Traci Paige Johnson,
Todd Kessler, and Angela C. Santomero as seen on Nick Jr.®

SIMON SPOTLIGHT
An imprint of Simon & Schuster Children's Publishing Division
1230 Avenue of the Americas, New York, New York 10020
Copyright © 2005 Viacom International Inc. All rights reserved.
NICKELODEON, NICK JR., *Blue's Clues*, and all related titles, logos, and characters are
trademarks of Viacom International Inc.
All rights reserved, including the right of reproduction in whole or in part in any form.
READY-TO-READ, SIMON SPOTLIGHT, and colophon are registered trademarks of
Simon & Schuster, Inc.
Manufactured in the United States of America
First Edition
2 4 6 8 10 9 7 5 3 1

Library of Congress Cataloging-in-Publication Data

Inches, Alison.
Hooray for Polka Dots! / by Alison Inches.—1st ed.
p. cm.—(Blue's clues. Ready-to-read; #10)
Based on the TV series Blue's Clues as seen on Nick Jr.
Summary: Blue's class goes to the fair, and when some of the rides seem too scary,
Polka Dots comes to the rescue.
ISBN 0-689-87210-0
[1. Dogs—Fiction. 2. Fairs—Fiction. 3. Fear—Fiction.] I. Title. II. Series.
PZ7.I355Hm 2005
[E]—dc22
2004008592

Hi! It is me,  .
Today I am going
to the fair
with my !

is coming

POLKA DOTS

with us.

I love to go places

with  !

POLKA DOTS

We are riding on
the  !
SCHOOL BUS
The  stops
SCHOOL BUS
at the fair  .
GATE

Wow! Look at all the rides!

MAGENTA wants to go on the AIRPLANE ride. PERIWINKLE wants to go on the MERRY-GO-ROUND.

I want to go on the giant .

SLIDE

But first we eat lunch.
We have  PIZZA and  JUICE .
Yum!

Now it is time for rides! Yay!

"Wow! The  go really high," says .

AIRPLANES

MAGENTA

"Hold on to  !"
POLKA DOTS

I say.

"Then the 🛩 will
AIRPLANES

not seem so high."

"Now I love the AIRPLANE

ride!"

says 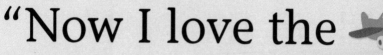 .

MAGENTA

"We love the  AIRPLANE
ride too!" say PERIWINKLE
and I.

"The  goes

MERRY-GO-ROUND

really fast,"

says  .

PERIWINKLE

"Hold on to  !"

POLKA DOTS

I say.

"Then the  will

MERRY-GO-ROUND

not seem so fast."

"Now I love the  !" says  .

MERRY-GO-ROUND   PERIWINKLE

"We love the

MERRY-GO-ROUND

too!" say  and I.

MAGENTA

"Now it is my turn!"
I say.
I want to ride the
giant .

SLIDE

Wow! That  sure
is tall!

SLIDE

"Hold on to !"

POLKA DOTS

say and  .

MAGENTA

PERIWINKLE

"Then the  will

SLIDE

not seem so tall."

Wheeeee!

"Now I LOVE the giant  !" I say.

SLIDE

"We do too!" say  and  .

PERIWINKLE   MAGENTA

Hooray for  !

POLKA DOTS